Raci CD Rocket

written by Lucinda Cotter

illustrated by Cherie Zamazing

a Capstone company—publishers for children

Engage Literacy is published in the UK by Raintree.
Raintree is an imprint of Capstone Global Library Limited, a company
incorporated in Engand and Wales having its registered office at 264
Banbury Road, Oxford, OX2 7DY – Registered company number: 6695582

www.raintree.co.uk

Written by Lucinda Cotter
Lead authors Jay Dale and Anne Giulieri
Cover illustration and illustrations by Cherie Zamazing
Edited by Gwenda Smyth
UK edition edited by Dan Nunn, Catherine Veitch and Sian Smith
Designed by Susannah Low, Butterflyrocket Design

Racing CD Rocket
ISBN: 978 1 406 26546 0
10 9 8 7 6 5 4

Printed and bound in the United Kingdom.

Contents

Chapter 1
The Race Is On

Josh opened the back door after school.

"Dad! Mum!" he shouted. "You'll never guess what we're doing at school! We're having a car race for Science Week. We can only use cars we have made ourselves. Can you help me build a racing car?"

"A racing car?" said Mum, looking puzzled.

"Yes," said Josh. "The cars must be powered by rubber bands. I've already planned my car." He showed them both the drawing he'd done at school.

"Wow!" said Dad. "This looks great. We can get started tomorrow."

Josh, Dad and Mum spent Saturday morning making the racing car. They used part of a cardboard box for the body. For the axles they used the outsides of four old pens. They slid two long thin ones inside two short fat ones. They used craft sticks to join it all together. Then Josh had a great idea! He decided to use old CDs for the wheels.

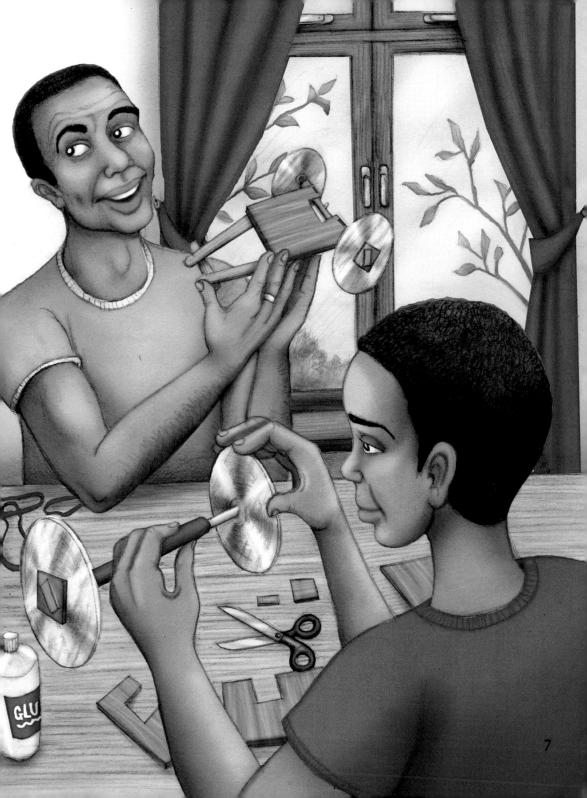

The most important part of the car was
a long rubber band. Josh looped the rubber
band around both ends of the back axle.
He then pulled it tight and looped it
twice around the front axle.

"We stretch the rubber band by turning the
back axle round and round," explained Dad.
"Then, when you let it go ..."

"ZOOOOM!" said Josh. "It'll go like a rocket!"

"A CD rocket," agreed Dad.

And that's what they called Josh's home-made
racing car — CD Rocket!

Chapter 2
A Problem

Josh took CD Rocket to school on Monday morning for a trial race.

"How did it go?" asked Dad, when he came to get Josh after school.

"It didn't go," said Josh, sadly. "That was the problem."

"I don't understand," said Dad, looking puzzled. "CD Rocket worked really well at home."

"It was the wheels," explained Josh. "They slipped on the shiny floor and wouldn't turn. Danny's car has huge rubber wheels. He calls it 'The Beast'. It beat CD Rocket by a long way."

"Don't give up," said Dad. He put his arm around Josh. "We'll think of something."

"Maybe we could get some big rubber wheels, too," suggested Josh. "I could take the wheels off one of my toy cars."

"It wouldn't be a CD Rocket, then, would it?" said Dad, smiling.

"I guess not," sighed Josh.

On the way to the car park, Dad saw some balloons dropped on the ground.

"What are these doing here?" he asked Josh.

"One of the other classes made rocket balloons today," explained Josh.

"Science Week sounds like a lot of fun," said Dad, "but I'd better put these balloons in the bin."

"No, wait!" cried Josh. "I have a better idea. We might be able to use them to fix CD Rocket."

When Dad and Josh arrived home, Josh got straight to work. He cut four circles from the balloons and stretched them around the CD wheels.

"They'll work just like tyres," he told Dad. "They'll grip the floor and stop the wheels from slipping."

"The CDs really look like wheels now," agreed Dad. "The only thing left to do is to try them out."

Josh and Dad decided to try the new wheels on the wooden floor in the living room. It was similar to the floor in the school hall where the cars would be raced.

"Ready for blast-off?" Dad asked.

Josh nodded and crossed his fingers as Dad let the rubber band go.

BING! ZOOOOM!
CD Rocket took off across the room in a straight line.

"Yahoo!" cried Josh. "The tyres work!"

MEEE-OW! There was a sharp screech as a ball of black fur leapt into the air and then disappeared under the dining table.

"Sorry, Sooty!" said Josh to his angry cat. "I didn't know you were there." Two green eyes glared at him from under the table.

Chapter 3
Ready, Set, Race!

Finally, it was race day. Everyone gathered in the school hall. A track had been marked out on the floor with tape. Josh stared at the finish line. It seemed a long way away.

There were five cars at the starting line. The Beast was next to CD Rocket. Danny grinned at Josh, but Josh was too nervous to smile. He carefully turned the back wheels until the rubber band was tight. CD Rocket was ready for blast-off.

"Racers, get ready!" shouted Mr Lew, their teacher. Everyone was suddenly quiet. Josh and the other racers bent over their cars.

"Ready! Set!" cried Mr Lew.

Josh held his breath.

"**Go!**" shouted Mr Lew.

WHOOOOSH! went The Beast.

ZOOOOM! went CD Rocket.

Everyone cheered as the cars raced across
the floor. The Beast roared! CD Rocket blasted!
One of the cars left the track and crashed into
the crowd. The Beast and CD Rocket were
very close. Heads turned as they flashed past.
They were way out in front of the other
cars. The Beast and CD Rocket were still
together as they crossed the finish line.

"It's a tie!" shouted Mr Lew. "We have two winners!" Mr Lew took Josh and Danny by the hands, and raised their arms in the air. "I think everyone did such a good job, we should have a car race like this every year!" he announced, happily.

"Are you upset that CD Rocket didn't beat The Beast?" asked Dad, when he picked Josh up after school.

"Not really," replied Josh. "We made a great car with some old CDs and a couple of balloons. But next year's car will be even better. We have a whole year to plan. The Beast won't stand a chance!"